Kitty Litter

For Audrie, Finn & August.
You three are so much more
than I could have ever imagined.

DIAL BOOKS FOR YOUNG READERS
An imprint of Penguin Random House LLC, New York

Copyright © 2020 by Vanessa Roeder

Visit us online at penguinrandomhouse.com

ISBN 9780735230507

Printed in China
10 9 8 7 6 5 4 3 2

Design by Jennifer Kelly
Text hand-lettered by Vanessa Roeder

This book was created with Prismacolor pencils, acrylic paint, and a boxful of digital tricks.

the B⬚X Turtle

by
Vanessa
Roeder

CRACK!—

Dial Books for Young Readers

When the little box turtle hatched, his parents noticed something missing.

But they weren't dismayed. They gave him a name and a shell, both of which fit just right.

Terrance's shell kept him dry on the soggiest days,

safe from the
snoopiest strangers,

and on the scariest nights...

it was big enough to share.

Terrance loved
his shell.

Suddenly, Terrance's shell seemed too boring,

too bizarre,

and too big for the little box turtle to bear.

So he abandoned it to search for
something better.

Terrance searched
high and low
until ...

His new shell looked sleek!

EEK!

But it showed
too much cheek.

The search
continued.

He looked classy.
He looked sassy.
He looked just like...

He looked for another shell.

He found it.

A perfect
polka-dotty
package...

that was
positively
petrifying!

Terrance tried shell,

after shell,

after shell,

after shell,

but nothing fit.

In that moment, the hermit crab showed what it meant to be a friend.

The little crustacean was so much more than just a shell.

And maybe Terrance was too.

Terrance knew
what he needed.

But when he found his old shell,

it had changed.

Terrance patched on soggy days.

He toiled on chilly nights.

The task grew big enough to share.

Finally, the shell was finished.

It wasn't sleek or sassy.

It was far from perfect and definitely

But Terrance wasn't dismayed,

because this little box turtle...

was so much more than just his shell.

the